Svensson Nore Junior

by

Linda Socha Jaworski

Illustrated by

Kirsten Karahan

Svensson Nore Junior
A Twinkle Truth Story

Author Linda Socha Jaworski
Illustrated by Kirsten Karahan

Twinkle Truth Publications
http://lindasochajaworski.org

ALL RIGHTS RESERVED. This book contains material protected under International and Federal Copyright Laws and Treaties. Any unauthorized reprint or use of this material is prohibited. No part of this book may be reproduced or transmitted in any form or by any means, electronic or mechanical, including photocopying, recording, or by any information storage and retrieval system without express written permission from the author/publisher.

*To Mike,
With love.*

By Linda Socha Jaworski

Tee's Gift
Tee's Song
Tee's Halloween
Tee's Treasure-True Forest
Jessie and the Tooth Fairy
The Seven Fairy Mountains of Cappadocia

Twinkle Truth Publications
Children's Literature

CONTENTS

	Acknowledgments	i
1	The Storm	08
2	The Mystery	24
3	Tromso	30
4	Svensson's Astonishment	38
5	Grandmother Jordforvert's Prophecy	46
6	Sven's Decision	52
7	The Journey Begins	60
8	Mother Bear's Miracle	66
9	The Auroras	74
10	Baby Bear's Decision	84
11	Three Parents	92
12	The Polar Almoner	98

Linda Socha Jaworski

*Thank you to Rich for
being a faithful reader.*

Thank you to Mike, and to Laura.

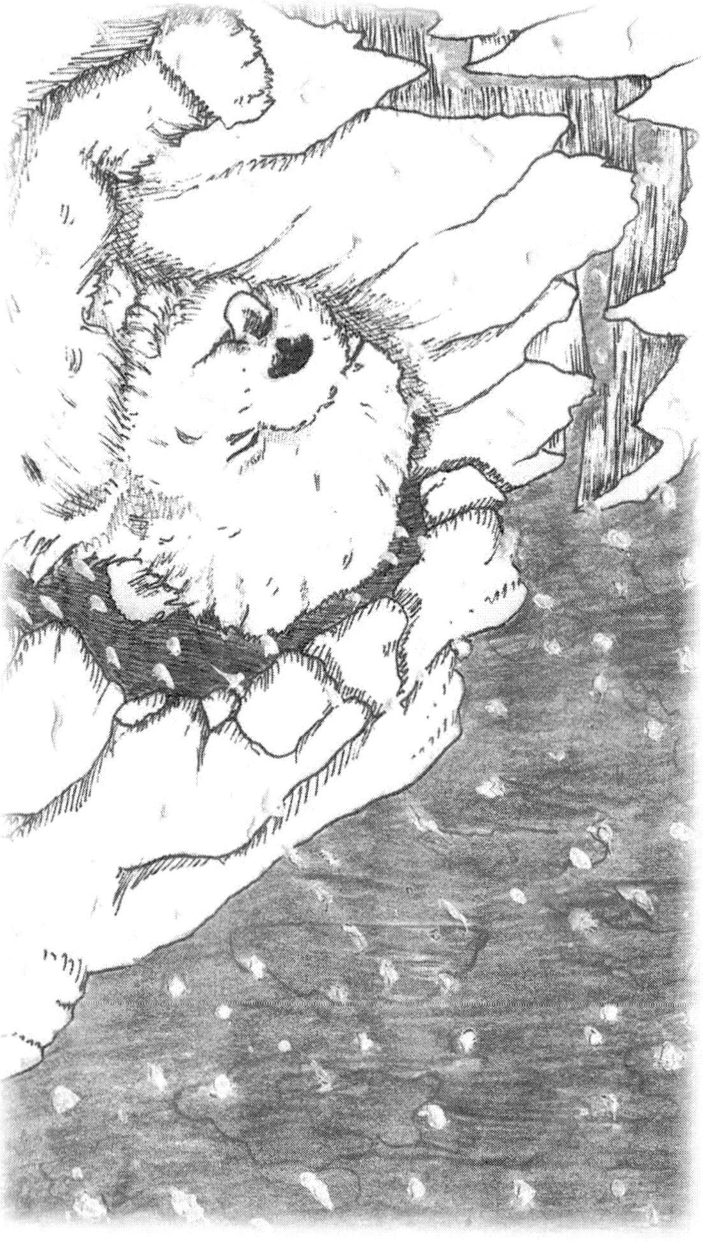

Chapter 1

The Storm

Once upon a time there was a mother Polar Bear, living on a lovely oasis of ice and snow, near the North Cape Plateau in Norway. She was the proud mother of a beautiful young cub.

This snowy morning in March was Baby Cub's third-month birthday. He awakened feeling very happy, as well as very hungry. While cuddling the cub, Mother Bear fed him and then she nudged him to rest and conserve his energy until she returned from her hunt for fresh ringed seal. She took the moment to gaze upon her little one. His soft white fur was beautiful, and then there were his eyes. She could not remember when she had ever seen a bear with green eyes. Pondering their color reminded her of something, but she could not think what it was. No matter, he was a treasure to be sure.

Mother Bear had lost much of her fat reserve, and she needed to eat soon. She had been in her birth-den with her cub for three months. During that time she had not eaten, nor drunk, nor left the cave. All Mother Bear did for three whole months was to feed and care for her baby!

Her baby needed sustenance to be healthy, and Mother Bear herself was very hungry too! Now she had no choice but to venture out for food and leave the little one on his own. She warned Kjærlighet, her cub, to stay in his safe environs at all times. Mother Bear explained to him that she would hunt as swiftly as was bearly possible and return with his supper that very day. It was the nature of bear cubs to remain in their cave dens for their first three months before venturing out into the snowy world. There was no worry about him wandering away, but Mother Bear felt better leaving him with that little reminder! After her gentle warning, she picked him up with her left paw, hugged him lovingly, and then placed him gently back into his snow crib.

Mother Bear's plan sounded just right to Baby Cub, so he snuggled himself into his snowy cave-home, well within the side of the small Arctic mountain. Kjærlighet drifted off to dreams of snowflakes, and of his dinner that would soon arrive! This would be his first taste of food, as until now he had only had his mother's milk. This was an exciting day indeed!

Mother Bear bounded away steadily, and began her hunt. She progressed more slowly than usual due to an annoying Arctic storm that began to brew. The squall wasn't quite in full force yet, so she gauged that she had time to grocery hunt and return to Kjærlighet well before earth-set, when twelve hours of darkness would engulf their snowy home.

Mother Bear made her way to the ice. It was more dangerous now that the winters were shorter than they had been in the past. The ice began to melt, and that presented her with a precarious situation: the ice was not as strong at this time of year as it had been earlier. This was because for some reason, winters were getting shorter and the ice was getting thinner. Mother Bear now had more trouble finding a safe place on the ice where she could wait for the much needed food. She had to be careful to bide her time on solid ice, which was becoming more and more difficult for her to find.

After a long search and burdened by high winds, she found a spot where she could still-hunt. She crouched in silence near the seal's small breathing hole in the ice. Mother Bear waited to grab the ringed seal with her giant left fore-paw when it came up for air. Her wait was tiring. Just when she thought she might have to return without food, a seal popped its head up to breathe. Mother Bear's Olympian speed reactions earned her a catch. Satisfied that she had been able to hunt successfully, Mother Bear held the food between her clenched jaws, and turned herself in the direction of her snow mountain cave-home.

Meanwhile a williwaw, a violent squall, zipped around the snow mountain where Kjærlighet lay nestled warm and secure. This powerful Arctic wind gathered strength, and blew millions of snowflakes to dancing everywhere! The williwaw whipped like steel scythes at the snowy mountain where Kjærlighet slept in his cave. Unknown to Mother Bear, she and Kjærlighet's mountain-home had weakened over the last year due to climactic changes. Now the williwaw tore at the mountain home with such force that a sound of thunder deafened Kjærlighet's ears! This fury of nature's energy shook the mountain as though it were a play toy in the hands of a giant.

The little one woke with a start, frightened by the uproar. The mountain quaked with a booming din he could never have imagined, and a violence that pushed him around in his cave as though he were a feather.

Kjærlighet screamed for his mother as the mountain itself seemed to roar as a perilous power, unparalleled in the Arctic. He wanted to run, but remembering Mor's words, he huddled, barely breathing, close to the farthest wall of his cave.

With thunderous sound and Achillean strength, propelled by this powerful force, the mountain split! One small part of his mountain-home, the part with Kjærlighet in his den, fell clamoring dangerously to the ocean! Because the ocean was not completely iced over, and there were still pockets of water everywhere, the newly formed small iceberg was blown, tossed about and pushed by the squall in all directions. Landing with a mighty thud into the icy Arctic, Mother Bear's den floated away, away, away.

Far from this tragedy and unknown to her, Mother Bear found herself in such horrific conditions that she was forced to seek shelter and wait out the storm. She searched for a very long time to find even a crevice within which she might shield herself from danger. Forceful winds were zapping her strength quickly! The poor bear was already in a gravely weakened state, not having eaten for the last three months. Nearing her last ounce of strength, she moved toward the upper side of a strong mountain, and used her razor sharp claws to quickly make a shelter for herself. She turned her back to the outside of her shallow refuge, and finally was able to take a moment to think through her situation.

Mother Bear knew she was in a predicament, and was very upset not being able to cuddle her precious one. There was only one small feeling of peace for Mother Bear; she knew that Baby Cub had a safe, warm nook carved out for himself. Their den kept him warm, and his coat had filled in nicely; he had enough fat to last until at least the day before she could return home. She made herself feel better thinking about the effort she had given to making a snug home for Kjærlighet; he would be safe from this daunting storm. But knowing things and feeling things are much different, and despair continually entered Mother Bear's mind. She pushed these thoughts from herself, deciding that perhaps her predicament was just too much for a new mother to take, and her imagination might be getting the best of her.

Unfortunately, this storm was one of the worst types, and it grew in strength rather than diminish. Hungry to the point of total exhaustion, Mother Bear was forced to eat her catch, which then strengthened her and made her feel better. She'd so wanted to return swiftly to Kjærlighet. This was not how she had intended her little Baby Cub to spend that day in his Arctic home! But after three months, she could have waited no longer; she had to have food for herself, or she would have had no strength left to hunt, ever again.

Two, long dreadful days passed as Mother Bear sheltered herself within that shallow snow crevice. She could not venture forth towards home as the force of the williwaws would have blown her even farther from Baby Cub. She stared at millions of white snowflakes flying, flurrying and scurrying every which way.

Now she was overwrought with fear. Although, she knew her child, like all bears, had an innate sense for survival, little Kjærlighet was only three months old and could not defend himself. Besides being hungry and alone, he needed nuzzling too! No mother wants her little one left on his own.

The following day brought the let-up of the storm she had hoped for, and she was finally able to begin her journey home. She saw opportunities for fresh needed catches, but didn't stop. She felt very compelled and propelled toward her little one. She needed food, but more importantly she felt an urgent need to check on her Baby Cub before hunting again. Mothers have ways of knowing things, and she had a foreboding feeling that gnawed at her innards. Mother Bear ached to snuggle her little Kjærlighet.

Linda Socha Jaworski

Chapter 2

The Mystery

After racing home at top speed, Mother Bear finally arrived at her den. She was completely perplexed, and filled with dread. Her home was gone! It had disappeared! No, she thought, she must be disoriented from the horrible experience of the last few days. Yet, search as she may, she could not find her den, and she noticed that her mountain-home was distinctly smaller than it was when she left just two and a half days ago. Mother Bear's mapping instincts confirmed that her den was gone! She frantically searched everywhere, but in vain. She screamed, searched more, and screamed again for her Kjærlighet, but there was no answer.

Mother Bear could not fathom what had happened! Her mind was filled with confusion and terror. The terrible storm had prevented her from protecting her little one. Mother Bear felt frozen, not from the cold, but from sorrowful-despair.

Unknown to her, young Kjærlighet was far from their Arctic home. He was floating on a chunk of snow mountain in the Arctic Ocean, slightly southward along the coast of Norway. Kjærlighet sailed away from his devoted, loving Mor, and the fresh Arctic air that greeted him upon his birth just three months ago.

Forlorn and beside herself with worry for her Baby Cub, Mother Bear lay down on the icy snow and cried and cried until she had no tears left. Her Love was gone, and she wondered how she could ever go on without him. Her little one needed her, and she needed him. Who would help him, feed him, and care for him?

She must search! Mother Bear must not despair, no, there was hope. She would not give up; she would find her Baby Cub! Mother Bear's plan was to hunt, rest, and regain her strength. Then she would spend every minute of her life searching, until she found her own Kjærlighet, her beautiful cub.

Mother Bear's ability to catch scents upon the air was amazing. A Polar Bear is an extraordinarily unique animal. Mother Bear's sense of smell was so acute, that she had the ability to smell prey more than 32 miles away.

She pointed her broad, black nose in all directions to catch the scent of her Baby Cub. With tears in her dark eyes, she found only a very faint and very distant trace of her baby, yet now, she knew he was alive.

Linda Socha Jaworski

Chapter 3

Tromso

Not so far down the coast of Norway was a wintry town called Tromso. The people of Tromso, too, were experiencing the very same winter storm that attacked from the North-north. It had moved along the coast southward toward Tromso, which was still very far north. The violence of the williwaw, now gusting fiercely in Tromso, had been driving Kjærlighet's little iceberg as well, nearer, nearer, nearer to this hunting town. Tromso was no place for a bear, of any size, age or color! The Nordic townsmen were hunters one, hunters all!

Kierka and Svensson Nore lived on the northernmost edge of town, slightly removed from the village itself. Because of the storm, Kierka locked heavy wooden shutters over the windows, and quickly corralled her reindeer safely into their modest barn. Once done, Kierka sat serenely near her oil lamp, knitting away, and thinking about how Svens would be held up in town for the night. Svens had left early that morning for supplies, and had not yet returned. That was best, she thought; she'd be a bit lonely, but better that Svens remain in town to be safe.

Just then, a loud cry pierced Kierka's thoughts. She sat straight up as chills flew up and down her spine. The cry sounded frightened and frantic, and came from outside, in the storm! Hurrying to the living room window, she opened the wooden shutters, and peered through the frosty glazed glass. Kierka could not see anything at all except millions of white snowflakes flying, flurrying and scurrying every which way. Searching the surrounding environs through her squinted eyes, she thought she saw something move near the shoreline. She wished Svens were home, so he could look as well. She knew she shouldn't go out, and forced herself to go back to her knitting. Just as Kierka picked up her knitting needles, again she heard a loud, desperate wailing. It sounded like a baby!

Quickly as humanly possible with no more thought of safety, Kierka put on her furry anorak and boots, grabbed her flashlight, and then pushed open the front door. Tightly gripping her flashlight she made her way through the icy flurries to the shore's edge, from where she thought the sound had come. There, curled up in a furry white ball was a baby bear, panting, shivering, and looking terrified. Knowing this little fellow wouldn't last long on his own in the storm, she scooped him up into her arms without an ounce of fear, and headed back to her cozy home that seemed a fortress from this storm. Once inside, she put him near the fire, and covered him with a wooly blanket. Instinctively, Kierka grabbed five fresh fishes from the larder and fed him immediately.

Kjærlighet had never eaten food before. In his three months of life, he had only had his mother's milk. This food tasted strange, but it helped him to regain strength. He ate slowly, and then began to feel better.

Kjærlighet wondered what kind of bear this one was. She was small and frail, with little hair. Yet, she was kind, like his Mor. Baby Cub decided he would safely wait for his Mor to come for him.

Svensson Nore Junior

Linda Socha Jaworski

Chapter 4

Svensson's Astonishment

Kjærlighet, being just a baby, hadn't learned to fear humans. He was curious, and somehow understood that this strange but kindly bear, in an equally strange but kindly den, meant him no harm.

After the young cub calmed, and warmed up, Kierka put him on her lap and rocked him. She sang lullabies while cuddling him. Soon Kjærlighet fell fast asleep in her arms. Kierka sat smiling at him, and felt very motherly, although she had never had her own child. This Baby Bear is precious, she thought. Kjærlighet snuggled against Kierka in such a way that showed he trusted her. Kierka felt so incredibly happy cradling the cub that she, too, fell asleep while rocking him. She dreamed sweet dreams of a little one, playing on the floor right in front of her rocking chair, not caring a bit that the child was somewhat furry!

The next morning, Kierka was awakened suddenly by Svensson as he opened the front door and slammed it shut. Kjærlighet was also awakened from the loud slamming noise at the same time. Kierka smiled at Svens when he came in; the cub stared at him with wide eyes. He thought that this animal was even bigger than the one holding him! Svens was aghast when he saw a Polar Bear nestled in his wife's arms, a man-eating Polar Bear!

Svensson sat down near Kierka, worried, but hoping for an understandable explanation. He listened intently as Kierka recounted the events of the previous evening. Kierka decided that Baby Bear was in need of parents, and that she and Svens would do just fine!

Svensson was dumbfounded, truly dumfounded. But, for a moment he was mesmerized by the cub's green eyes. He did not know that a Polar Bear could have green eyes. Kierka hadn't noticed how the cub looked, only that he was a baby. Svens looked sympathetically at his wife and said, "My dear, you have a baby who might eat you one day! He will grow taller than our front door and we will never have enough money to feed him! No friend would dare venture near our home while we house a Polar Bear. How, how could this work?" wailed Svens.

Then, Svens's next thought brought wonder to Kierka too! Svens continued, "Kierka, haven't you wondered how he got here? He is far from his Arctic home! And, he is so young, a baby! Where is his mother?"

The two stared at each other as they mulled over this question. Kierka stood up, still holding her cub, and went to the window. She opened the shutter, and could see the small iceberg near the water's edge. Kierka saw the den carved it its side too. It seemed to be the birth place of the cub. Yet while her eyes told her this, she could not understand the truth of it. It was so impossible, yet he was here, with her and Svens. The night before she had not noticed any of this, because of the horrific storm, she had only seen the cub crying for help.

Kierka called Svens to the window, to look. They were perplexed. A small iceberg had delivered a Polar Bear cub to just about their front door. The two agreed that this was a mystery, and wondered where was the baby cub's mother?

Svensson Nore Junior

Linda Socha Jaworski

Chapter 5

Grandmother Jordforvert's Prophecy

Kierka pleaded, "Svens, last night as I held him, I was dreaming about him and he looked like a little boy. Something in the dream, a green swish, made me remember a story Grandmother Jordforvert told me once. I went to visit her when she was ill. We were in the sitting room, and I saw a beautiful green box in her china cabinet. The box had three white mountains painted on the top center of it; the largest of the three mountains stood in front, and two smaller ones were slightly behind. On the front of the box was a white clasp that was cut from a mother of pearl shell. I got up to look at it and found it odd that the clasp looked like a little tooth! Most amazing though, was the green. The color made it seem magical somehow.

Grandmother smiled at me and told me that one day she would send it to me. Then, she said that she had wanted to tell me something that should be shared with those you love, because this is the spirit of the lore: love. She said that each Nordic person can claim one moment for one wish if it is for love. To make the claim, you must be near the Auroras when green is dominant. If I claim Baby Bear for us, he will be little Svens. Baby Bear loves me, I can feel it!!"

"Kierka," Svens began gently, "This is only Grandmother Jordforvert's lore. We have no proof that this is true. How could we wish for such a miracle? It is so difficult to believe it could happen! But, you say green? Have you noticed his eyes?"

Kierka looked upon the Baby Cub, and was breathless for a moment. She could not believe the beautiful green of the little one's eyes. They were similar to the green in her dream. So touched in her heart by all that had happened, she could only say, "Oh Svens."

Nevertheless, Svens too, began to sense a gentle spirit in the little cub. It was true that they had not been blessed with a child, and they were already in their mid-life. Gazing upon his wife, newly transformed by caring for the cub, Svens wanted to believe in this lore, for Kierka, and for himself as well.

Svens began to think that maybe they should go to the Aurora Borealis. Lore often did have truth in it, he realized. Love, Svens believed was stronger than lore. He studied Baby Cub's gentle face. Surprisingly, he saw that the bear looked upon Kierka with love in his little green eyes. The affectionate ball of fur did seem very contented snuggled in Kierka's arms, just like a human child would, and in such a short time! It was almost as though the cub had been there, with them, long ago.

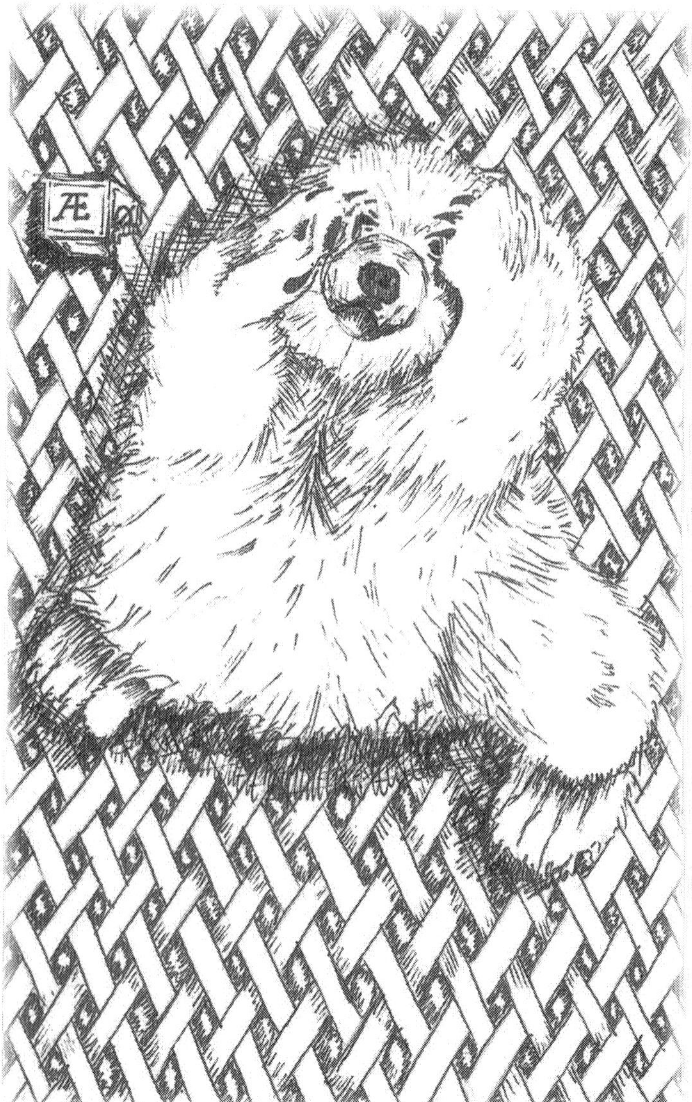
Æ

Chapter 6

Svens's Decision

Svens decided aloud, "The Spring Equinox is the time when the green aurora may dominate. We'll travel north! We will go to the auroras! We will make our wish! But, if Baby Cub remains a cub, Kierka, you must promise me that we'll take him back to his Arctic home. For his sake, he is much safer there than he would be if he were to remain here with us, in our hunting town of Tromso."

Kierka readily agreed, "I promise!"

It would be three whole weeks until the Spring Equinox! Kierka was eager to teach Baby Cub human ways. Eating cooked meat didn't work, he molded it like play dough; so she fed him raw fish, and that was better! Holding a fork didn't work, he raked the rug with it, so she allowed paws for the time being. Sitting on a chair did work because he turned it into a jungle gym and climbed, so she allowed eating while sitting on the floor. Sleeping in a bed didn't work, he always got underneath, and there she let him stay! Taking a bath didn't work, his hair seemed waterproof, and he just kept trying to swim in the tub which Kierka decided was good exercise and good play too! Building with blocks didn't work; he kept trying to eat them, and when that didn't work, he threw them at the ceiling and laughed at the noise it made; she decided rubber toys might be better. Brushing his teeth didn't work, he kept spitting the toothpaste at the wall just so he could lick it off! One thing did work though, hugs! When Kierka hugged Baby Cub, he hugged her back and he was strong! Together mother and baby contentedly learned each other's ways.

The three weeks passed quickly because Kierka was busy! Having a baby bear did take a lot of time, and so not much else got done. The house was a mess; less food was cooked, and the laundry piled sky high. But, there was happiness.

When the eve of three nights before the equinox finally arrived, Kierka felt a bit apprehensive. She'd made a promise to Svensson, but could she keep it? She loved Baby Cub so much already that the thought of parting from him made her feel as though the world would vanish! Yet, she did promise. Because she loved this little bundle of white fur so much, she knew she would only ever want what was best for him. He had grown so much already! He even tried saying words! They sounded more like little roars, but each roar had its own ring. Kierka was beginning to understand what he wanted by his self-created baby-talk.

A small 'r-r-r' meant 'ocean.' Baby Cub loved to sit and watch the ocean. A big 'r-r-r-r-r' meant 'hungry.' He said this most often throughout the day. A soft 's-s-s' meant 'snuggle.' Like all babies, he needed snuggle time. A 't-t-t' meant 'play.' He now had a few favorite games: peek-a-boo, patty-cake, and building. And, a 'k-k-k' meant 'Kierka.' She liked that word-sound the most! Baby Cub called for her as often as any child calls for his mom: very often!

Svensson Nore Junior

Linda Socha Jaworski

Chapter 7

The Journey Begins

It was two days before the Spring Equinox Day, and 6:00 am; the Nore family was up, and eager to begin their journey. Svensson had packed plenty of food, mostly fresh fish, all neatly arranged in a sturdy cold-weather backpack. Just as they stood at the threshold of their cottage, Kierka waited a moment and ran back to her room. She had saved one of Svensson's boyhood outfits of Nordic national dress. Svensson's mother loved this outfit that had marked a special day in Svensson's boyhood, and so she'd passed it on to Kierka. She grabbed the folded packet of warm, decorative clothing, and stuffed it into her sidebag. Kierka chose to believe in the magic of the lore, in the magic of love, and in her feelings.

The Nores quickly made their way to the dock to board the Nordnorde, which was navigating North to their destination at the tip of Norway, called North Cape Plateau. They would reach the Northern Lights in plenty of time.

Fortunately, Baby Cub was always sleepy in the morning. To begin this journey, he was tucked inside Svensson's huge backpack. It might not sound like fun being in a backpack, but Svens had rigged it so that it was quite nice in there. He had cut special air holes, three on each side; a piece of soft blanket was sewn into the wall of the backpack, just where the cub's chin would rest; a little pillow was placed in the bottom where the cub could sit comfortably, and Svens reworked the top flap of the backpack so that it stood up about three inches before folding over. That way Baby Cub could see where he was going. There, Kjærlighet slept like a log, well fed and secure!

Once on board the ship, Kierka and Svens settled in their modest cabin for the nearly two-day journey. It was good that they had arranged for that too, as the cub soon awakened, ready for play, and lots of fish! It was a full-time job keeping him busy in that small space, so they taught him to play Connect Four and he loved it. Kierka and Svens wore themselves out wrestling, dancing, and singing to Baby Cub. They were amazed at how he began to take interest in songs that just weeks ago would not occupy his attention at all! Kierka and Svens were so in love with Baby Cub, and he so in love with them, one would never know that they weren't his parents, except for the fact that he was a Polar Bear.

Linda Socha Jaworski

Chapter 8

Mother Bear's Miracle

Finally, the ship blew three loud whistles hailing their destination at the northernmost point of Norway. Eager to disembark, Kierka wanted to run to the wishing place called Aurora Summit, as her anticipation grew in her heart of hopes that soon she would have her baby!

Not far away another mother, still in pain for the loss of her newborn cub, smelled the air. Her keen sense told her that her own little cub was near! She had been searching nonstop as she had planned and now, with renewed hope, she followed the faint scent as well as she could. She realized she was moving a bit far from safe environs, but her zeal to find Kjærlighet was all that mattered. A mother never forgets her child.

Sensing Kjærlighet, she stood very still on her hind legs, her eight and half feet height reaching high into the air, while giving all of herself to holding onto his very familiar scent. Her spine tingled, her heart beat rapidly, she was certain that her own baby was nearby. Mother Bear ran toward the scent as her anticipation grew in her heart of hopes that soon she would have her baby.

Hurrying from the ship, the Nore family boarded the Aurora Line Bus. Svens and Kierka were now only 20 minutes from their wishing-place destination. But the problem they had was to keep Baby Cub inside Svens' backpack.

Kjærlighet sniffed the air and he, too, sensed familiarity. Baby Cub was confused; he recognized something he had missed, had cried for and desperately needed. He wiggled to let Svens know he would like to leave the backpack! Kierka patted his back again and again to calm him for the ride.

Mother Bear fervently watched the port; she saw humans and bustling activity near the disembarkation area of the ship. She could not see her child, but she was positive Baby Cub was there. She waited patiently, camouflaged near a snowy mountain. Time she had, and a goal she had as well – to rescue her little one. Sharp eyesight helped her catch a glimpse, yes, it was just a glimpse, but she was certain that she'd seen a small white paw on the back of a human. Confusion exploded in her brain thinking of such an impossibility! Mother Bear saw the human board the bus, and knew it would be tough to track him. But she would do it; she would jog along through the mountains, maintaining her distance, yet keeping pace with the bus. Fortunately for her, she'd eaten her fill of fresh Nordic ringed seal that very morning.

Jog, Mother Bear did! It was no easy feat. For some reason, she wasn't up to her usual speed. Emotion gave way to inner strength though, and helped her sustain the race with the bus. She had been on this quest for a little over three weeks. She would not allow anything to stop her now! She would find her child, her own Kjærlighet.

Svensson Nore Junior

Linda Socha Jaworski

Chapter 9

The Auroras

Once on board the bus, Kierka's hand was inside the backpack rubbing Baby Cub's neck. That kind gesture relaxed the cub, and he rested a bit easier. He seemed so unsettled all of a sudden. Perhaps it was a child's curiosity to want to see everything, Kierka thought. She hoped people would think it was a pet dog, but if that paw didn't stay inside, they would be found out for sure!

The bus driver called out, "Next stop, Auroras Special Lookout Summit, Northern Lights! The bus will return in one hour. You have a coffee shop to your left, and the trail to the Summit on the right."

Mother Bear stood high above the Aurora Summit stop, glaring at Svensson Nore. The pack bulged, and the bulge had a shape she recognized! Baby Cub was in that pack. Mother Bear could not grasp what the humans were doing with her baby; she must protect him! Surveying the area, she decided how to shadow the kidnappers. She saw that the Nores separated from the group when they exited the bus, and were alone on a trail leading toward an even more remote area, near the brightest point of lights, a lookout point. Mother Bear knew exactly where they were headed. From her perch she could see a parallel trail to track them, and still remain camouflaged; if only she weren't so tired, it would be so much easier. Mother Bear was prepared to fight for her baby, and she held no fear of such weak human animals. She resolved that she would leave this spot with Kjærlighet, her baby, this very day, this very moment!

His scent was coming to her on the winds, the chill, cold winds of the North, and her heart was warm and filled with hope, for what she longed for, for what was hers!

Kierka and Svensson hurried excitedly along the trail. They could not believe their luck! They were alone! The others needed warm drinks before trekking to the Aurora Summit. There was no need for Kierka and Svens to grab cocoa or coffee. Their hearts were warm, filled with so much hope and excitement. In both of their hearts, they yearned for success as the thought of leaving Baby Cub here was more than they could bear.

Within minutes, Kierka and Svens were facing the Auroras, were in the Auroras, and were through the Auroras, as the sky, itself, was the Aurora. The beauty was more than words could ever express. One must experience this to know it and believe it. Your senses tell you one thing, your heart another, but all of you together knows that life's essence is here, in this magical place. Life created by nature, and the nature of this aurora brought tingles of anticipation for their appeal;

they hoped so, that Grandmother Jordforvert was right!

Kierka lifted Baby Cub out of the backpack, heavy as he was. Her smile was greater than Svensson had ever seen, and the cub hugged her tightly as he, too, was amazed by their surroundings. Baby Cub's senses were on full alert as he sensed another known presence, something wonderful! Her scent! He knew this Mor! He felt unsure and confused, yet so happy.

The three stood facing the aurora. Kierka was holding Baby Cub's right hand, and Svensson was holding the left paw. The three faced the bright

Auroras, and the green was indeed dominant. At that perfect moment, Kierka opened her mouth to express their wish, when a ROAR louder than anything they had ever heard in their entire lives, surrounded them. It was ferocious, angry, threatening and fearless! The three stood frozen! Seconds felt like hours, and yet each one knew that the Roar must be faced.

As each Nore searched within for courage, the three slowly turned around, and faced Mother Bear, all eight and one-half feet of her! Mother Bear was wailing and waving her ferocious arms in pure fury and rage. Svens,

Kierka, and Baby Cub felt her agony as well as their own. All four were filled with fear, apprehension and complete confusion. While these feelings registered within each, time stood still for a moment and no one moved.

Svensson Nore Junior

Linda Socha Jaworski

Chapter 10

Baby Bear's Decision

After a few frozen moments, Baby Cub let go of Kierka and Svens's hands. He took two steps toward his Mother Bear and stopped. Mother Bear stood silently, lovingly gazing upon her cub. She saw immediately that he'd been well taken care of, and he was very contented. She felt perplexed and could not understand what had happened; how could her precious baby be with brutal humans, here, in her Arctic home?

Kierka's heart was torn; she knew this was Baby Cub's mother, and she also understood that this moment in time would never repeat itself. Kierka felt great sorrow-shame to want another mother's child, but her love for this little one would allow her nothing less than to make her wish in the green of the aurora.

Kierka looked longingly at Svens, wishing he had an answer for her thoughts that bounced back and forth between each other, tugging at her; guilt for taking the child, yet great love for knowing he should be with her.

Svens knew exactly what her look meant; he felt it too. He did not want to hurt Mother Bear, nor Baby Cub. He wondered how they could have come to this point. They were here, in the auroras, holding this young cub's hands and facing his terrified mother. He and Kierka were separating them, this was her baby. Yet, he too, felt the force of their hope, their love and could not stop himself from wanting to make the wish.

They gently took Baby Cub's hands back. The cub didn't pull free, but he did stay close to his Bear Mother! In the moment when Kierka yearned to make the wish, the Baby gained wisdom, insight; he knew truth. He realized Mother Bear was with cub. He understood Mother Kierka would never have a cub. He loved both mothers, and he understood that they both loved him too.

But, his thoughts focused on his destiny, understanding the way. Something deep inside of him helped him to understand that love came in many ways to the world, and that he must use love to allow himself to be part of this wish, the wish that would change his life, his Mor's life, and Kierka and Svens's lives too.

Mother Bear could feel her little one thinking; she waited, and remembered. As she gazed upon her little Kjærlighet with his bright green eyes, she recalled an ancient Polar lore; her mother had passed this lore to her, long ago. Her own mother had explained that a 'descendant-innocent soul' called, The Polar Almoner, would one day prevent the probable extinction of their race. The Almoner would be a bear-man. The story was repeated for ages, and no one had ever understood this lore at all. A human is human, and a bear is a bear. No one could fathom how the two races would mix, from innocence, until now.

Her Kjærlighet! He was different. Mother Bear began to understand; bears did not have green eyes; bears did not trust humans; bears were bears. She had even named him appropriately, for Kjærlighet means love.

For her race, for her cub's destiny, for life, she would find the way; the way to accept her greatest loss, and give Baby Cub her blessing, so that he may fulfill his destiny. Her love for him allowed this.

Baby Cub embraced his mother's blessing, then permitted himself to accept his destiny. Bravely, he slowly backed up a bit more toward Svens. Kierka felt Baby Cub's peace which was all that was needed for her confidence in her greatest desire. She solemnly whispered,

"Wishes are only wishes,
Unless they come from the heart.
In the green of this Aurora,
From our son, we wish to never part."

Linda Socha Jaworski

Chapter 11

Three Parents

The Auroras flared! The Green One grew! Svensson, Kierka, Kjærlighet and Mother Bear stood in amazement, mesmerized. The Aurora almost had a life of its own. It was beautiful, powerfull, beyond one's thinking. Then, a swirl, a large, soft swirl, came gently toward them and all four were enfolded. The Green enveloped them, caressed them, held them; tranquility prevailed. They were experiencing the Green, feeling its wonderment. Then, just as gently and slowly, the Green Aurora swirled its way back to the whole. The four Nordics stood motionless, entranced, in awe. The four were connected, but separated, forever and always.

Then, a very small voice was heard, "Mor." Svensson, Kierka and Mother Bear looked down. Sitting on the frozen Arctic floor was a naked child, yet warm, warm from whom he was, for whom he had become; Kjærlighet's inner self filled with aurora warmth; in this moment, no harm would come to him. This child, with white hair matching Mother Bear's coat, and green eyes matching the Green Aurora's green, held a visage of total peace. Kjærlighet gazed upon his parents intently, yet contentedly. All three parents watched as the child picked up a small thing from the ground.

Kierka's eyes welled with tears. She hugged the child pulling him inside of her winter coat while saying, "Svensson hurry, take the clothing from my side-bag!"

Mother Bear's eyes welled with tears too. Her son was human, but his hair was still hers! Though tears fell, Mother Bear was at peace. In her nature and for nature, she allowed her child to make his own choice. Finding it difficult to leave him, nonetheless, she took one step toward her trail and turned for one last look at her child.

The little Polar Almoner was walking wobbily toward her. She waited and watched with joy in his every step. When near to her, he pointed at her middle. She put her paw there in response, and at the moment her paw touched her middle, a small paw from her inside met her paw on the outside, another cub! Mother Bear wondered how it could be possible that her little Almoner realized this.

Linda Socha Jaworski

Chapter 12

The Polar Almoner

Mother Bear had never felt complete well-being, and complete sad-peace at the same time. She put her left paw out to her child, Kjærlighet, for one last touch. The Polar Almoner touched her paw with respect and love, and then hugging her said, "Mor, jeg elsker deg."

Afraid of hurting her now fragile cub, she did not embrace her sweet child, but smiled her blessing upon him in Bear language. Caringly and kindly, Mother Bear left her child, and disappeared in a moment as she soon camouflaged into the Arctic environs. Kierka and Svens held their hands up to her, and bid her truly well and farewell.

Little Svens seemed about four years old. His parents dressed him, double checked his zippers and buttons, each took a hand, and stood facing the Auroras. They each said in their hearts what they did, and that is for each of them to know.

The Aurora Summit Coffee Shop was waiting for them at the top of the path. Svens led the trio toward the shop, but little Svens pointed forwards, past the shop. He showed that he wanted to climb up a trail, to a small mountain's perch. There were three mountains directly in front of them, past the trail. One was larger in the front, and there were two smaller mountains, one on each side of the large one. Svens stopped for a moment and stared at this landscape. It seemed so familiar, but he felt that impossible.

Then, Svens wondered if the child wanted to see his Mor, and so he allowed the little one to lead them. Once at the top, little Svens stood peering out into the world. His face looked curious and happy.

Little Svens could see many miles into the distance and a small white speck was there; he focused on this. A moment later, she felt, she turned and then saw her son; they locked the moment, a moment to keep. The little one whispered upon the icy wind: "Farvel, inntil vi møtes igjen." The child heard her whisper back and nodded. Then, little Svens Jr. smiled and pointed. Kierka followed the direction of his little finger, but only saw the Arctic environs, beautiful as they were. Svens thought the little one was finding the site of the Arctic, with different eyes.

The breeze brought scents of Arctic life to the Almoner. As he watched the distance, he felt life flowing through the earth beneath his feet. In this time of feelings, he stood experiencing himself; he felt his parents too. Looking up to find both Kierka and Svens gazing down at him with wonder and awe in their eyes, smiling their feelings toward him, he felt the human.

Warmth, good and pure; he was shielded with an essence of life converging from many forms, each to compliment the other.

Smiling up to his parents, he said, "I am Svensson Jr." Filled with joy, they knelt to hug him tightly. Then, Kierka said, "Come my little Svensson Jr. Your first taste of warm cocoa awaits you."

The three descended toward the Aurora Summit Coffee Shop. There was a new smell coming from the little cafe down below for Svens Jr. to experience.

Soon enough, little Svens was peering in through the window at the pots of steamy drinks behind the counter. He was curious and eager to try hot cocoa. Svens smiled at Svens Jr. and opened the door. Then, with a wink, he said, "Svens Jr., today we have a reason to celebrate. A proper celebration always includes chocolate! We will order mugs of hot cocoa and toast life."

Young Svens smiled back at his father as they sat in a warm, comfortable booth, eagerly awaiting the treat. The three sat together smiling ear to ear, and sipping their cocoa with cinnamon cookies. This birthday was one to remember.

Did the Nores live happily ever after? Well of course, we all do! But, there are many more tales to tell of young Svensson Nore Jr.!

Farvel, inntil vi møtes igjen!

Norwegian Translations

Farewell, until we meet again.
Farvel, inntil vi møtes igjen.

Mother, I love you.
Mor, jeg elsker deg.

Kjærlighet (Sha-lee-et)
Love

Svensson Nore
Sven-son Nur-ah

Jordforvert
Jurd-fer-vetch

Made in the USA
Lexington, KY
27 September 2012